DETROIT PUBLIC LIBRARY

P9-DIH-201

Snow Valentines

by Karen Gray Ruelle

CHASE BRANCH LIBRARY
17731 W. SEVEN MILE RD.
DETROIT, MI 48235
578-8002

Holiday House / New York

APR   2014

CH

to my valentine

Copyright © 2000 by Karen Ruelle
All Rights Reserved
Printed in the United States of America
Reading Level: 2.5

Library of Congress Cataloging-in-Publication Data
Ruelle, Karen Gray.
Snow valentines / by Karen Ruelle.—1st ed.
p. cm.
Summary: Harry and his sister, Emily, want to make
an original valentine for their parents but cannot seem
to find the right idea, until a surprise snowstorm inspires them.
ISBN 0-8234-1533-3 (hardcover)
ISBN 0-8234-1782-4 (paperback)
[1. Valentine's Day—Fiction. 2. Snow—Fiction.] I. Title
PZ7.R88525 Sn 2000
[E]—dc21   99-046315

Contents

1. The Best Hugs and Pictures

Harry's mother gave the best hugs
in the world.
She gave hello hugs.
She gave good-bye hugs.
She gave thank-you hugs.
When Harry was happy,
she gave him happy hugs.
When Emily was sad,
she gave her extra happy hugs
to cheer her up.
Harry's mother's hugs were the best.

Harry's father drew the best pictures
in the world.

He drew pictures on napkins.

He drew pictures on letters.

He drew pictures for Harry and Emily
for their birthdays.

When Emily was silly,

he drew her silly pictures.

He even drew pictures and

put them in Harry's lunch box.

Harry's father's pictures were the best.

Now it was February.

Valentine's Day was in two weeks.

Harry knew his mother

would give Valentine's Day hugs.

Harry knew his father

would draw Valentine's Day pictures.

Harry knew they would be

the best hugs and best pictures.

Harry wanted to give
his mother and father
a valentine, too.
He asked Emily,
"What can we do for Valentine's Day?"
"We can cut out red paper hearts,"
said Emily.
Harry shook his head.
"Everyone cuts out red paper hearts."

"We can write 'I love you' on a card,"
  said Emily.

"Everyone writes 'I love you' on a card.
  I want it to be something
  no one else will do.
  I want something just from me."

"And from me, too," said Emily.

"Yes, from you, too," said Harry.

2. Awful, Horrible, Yucky Valentines

Harry and Emily thought
about valentines.
They thought and thought.
"I know," said Emily.
"Let's make up
a Valentine's Day dance."
Harry and Emily went upstairs.
They shut the door.

"We can start like this," said Emily.

She jumped up and down three times.

"Then we can do this," she said.

She stomped her feet.

She waved her arms around.

"They will like this dance," said Emily.

Harry and Emily practiced together.

They stomped their feet.

They waved their arms around.

"Now we have to spin," said Emily.

They both spun until they were dizzy.

They fell down.

"They will like this dance,"
said Harry.

Then there was
a knock at the door.

"What is all
that awful thumping?"
asked their mother.

"I know," said Harry.

"Let's make up

a Valentine's Day song, instead.

It can start like this."

Harry started to sing

a Valentine's Day song.

He sang in a loud voice.

Emily sang, too.

They sang and they sang.

The song got louder and louder.

"I think they will really like this song,"

said Emily.

After ten verses,

there was a knock on the door.

"What is all that horrible noise?"

asked their father.

15

"I know," said Emily.

"Let's make up

  a Valentine's Day dessert."

"I think they will really like that,"

  said Harry.

  They went into the kitchen.

  Their mother was making dinner.

"Mom, may we please have

  the applesauce?"

  said Harry.

"And the peanut butter?" said Emily.

"And the marshmallows?" said Harry.

"Yuck," said their mother.

"I hope you aren't going to mix them
  all together."

"Never mind,"
  said Harry and Emily together.

3. Snow Day

It was the day before Valentine's Day.

Harry woke up early.

He looked out the window.

"Look!" he shouted to Emily.

"Look at the snow!"

"There is no school today,"

said their mother.

"It is a snow day."

"Hooray!" shouted Harry and Emily.

Harry and Emily played in the snow
all day long.

They made a snowman.

They made a snowwoman.

They made a whole snow family.

They even made snow pets.

After lunch, they made a snow house
for their snow family.

It looked like a snow fort.

They filled it with snowballs.

Then they had a big snowball fight
with the snow family.
Harry and Emily won.
It was getting dark.
Harry and Emily came inside.

"You two make the best snow people,"
said their mother.
"That's true," said their father.
"I've never seen a better snowman."

At bedtime, Harry remembered
about Valentine's Day.
"Oh, no," he said to Emily.
"Tomorrow is Valentine's Day.
We still don't have a valentine."
"Maybe we will dream an idea,"
said Emily.

Their mother tucked them in.

She gave them good-night kisses.

Harry's father said good-night, too.

Then it was quiet.

"What will we do?"

whispered Harry.

4. The Very Best Valentines

All night, it snowed and it snowed.

All night, Harry and Emily

dreamed of valentines.

The next morning,

there was lots of new snow.

"Another snow day," said Harry.

He jumped out of bed.

It was very early.

"Emily, wake up," he said.

"Look at all the snow!"

Emily looked outside.

But she was not happy.

"Today is Valentine's Day.

We have no valentines,"

she said sadly.

"All we have is snow."

Harry looked at Emily.

"That's it!" he said.

They put on their hats and scarves.

They ran out into the snow.

They made great big snow hearts.

They drew hearts in the snow.

They wrote "I love you" in the snow.

By the time they finished,

breakfast was ready.

"Look outside," Harry and Emily said.

"Happy Valentine's Day!"

Harry's father looked outside.

"Snow valentines," he said.

"They are so wonderful.

Thank you."

He smiled at Harry and Emily.

"Happy Valentine's Day," he said.

He gave them each

a beautiful Valentine's Day picture.

Harry's mother
looked outside.
"You two made
the best
snow valentines
in the world.

"Happy Valentine's Day,"
she said.
And she gave
them each
a great, big
Valentine's Day hug.

And after breakfast,
Harry and Emily
and their mother
and their father
went outside.
All together
they made a snow fort.
And they had
the best Valentine's Day
snowball fight ever.